OWLY

by Mike Thaler

Pictures by David Wiesner

Walker and Company ✺ New York

Published by Harper & Row, Publishers, Inc., in
1982. First published in paperback in 1998 by
Walker Publishing Company, Inc.

Published simultaneously in Canada by Thomas
Allen & Son Canada, Limited, Markham, Ontario.

Library of Congress Cataloging-in-Publication Data
Thaler, Mike, 1936–
Owly/by Mike Thaler; pictures by David Wiesner.
         p.   cm.
Summary: When Owly asks his mother question
after question about the world, she finds just the
right ways to help him find the answers.
ISBN 0-8027-7545-4 (pbk.)
[1. Owls—Fiction. 2. Parent and child—Fiction.]
I. Wiesner, David, ill. II. Title.
PZ7.T3Pw 1998
[E]—dc21   98-10682
                                              CIP
                                              AC

PRINTED IN HONG KONG

2 4 6 8 10 9 7 5 3

For Laurel Lee, my bride. —M.T.

Owly started asking questions
when he was two years old.
He would sit all night with his mother
under the stars.

"How many stars are in the sky?"
he asked one night.

"Many," answered his mother.

"How many?" asked Owly, looking up.

His mother smiled. "Count them."

"One, two, three, four…"

"One hundred and one,
  one hundred and two,
  one hundred and three,
  one hundred and four…"

Owly was still counting
when the sun came up.
"One thousand and one,
one thousand and two…"

"How many stars are in the sky?"
asked his mother.

"More than I can count," said Owly, blinking.
And he tucked his head under his wing,
and went to sleep.

The next night
Owly looked up at the sky again.
"How high is the sky?" he asked his mother.
"Very high," she said, looking up.
"How high?" asked Owly.
"Go and see," said his mother.

So Owly flew up into the sky.

He flew high above his tree.

He flew to the clouds.

He flapped his wings very hard.

He flew above the clouds.

But as high as he could fly,

the sky was always higher.

In the morning when he landed on the tree,
he was very tired.

"How high is the sky?" asked his mother.

"Higher than I can fly," said Owly,
closing his eyes and falling asleep.

The next night Owly heard the sound
of the waves in the ocean.
"How many waves are there in the ocean?"
he asked his mother.
"Many waves," she answered.
"How many?" asked Owly.

"Go and count them," she replied.

So Owly flew to the shore.

He stood on the beach and counted the waves.

"One, two, three, four…"

But as many as he could count,

many more followed.

"One thousand and one,

one thousand and two…"

And when the sun came up, he saw

that there was still an ocean full of waves.

So, sleepily, he returned to his mother.

"How many waves are in the ocean?" she asked.

"More than I can count," answered Owly,
closing his eyes.

The next night Owly asked his mother,

"How *deep* is the ocean?"

"Very deep," she answered.

"How deep?" asked Owly.

His mother looked out at the sky.

"Almost as deep as the sky is high," she said.

Owly looked up. He sat there all night
thinking about the sky, and the stars,
and the waves, and the ocean,
and all he had learned from his mother.

And as the sun came up he turned to her
and said, "I love you."
"How much?" asked his mother.
"Very much," answered Owly.
"How much?" she asked.
Owly thought for a minute
and then gave her a hug.
"I love you as much as the sky is high
and the ocean is deep."

She put her wing around him
and gave him a hug.
"Do you have any more hugs to give me?"
asked Owly.
"Many more." His mother hugged him again.
"How many more?" asked Owly, falling asleep.
"As many as there are waves in the ocean
and stars in the sky."

And she did.